LEO * LUKAS

The Magic Sword

Written and Illustrated By
Rosaria L. Calafati

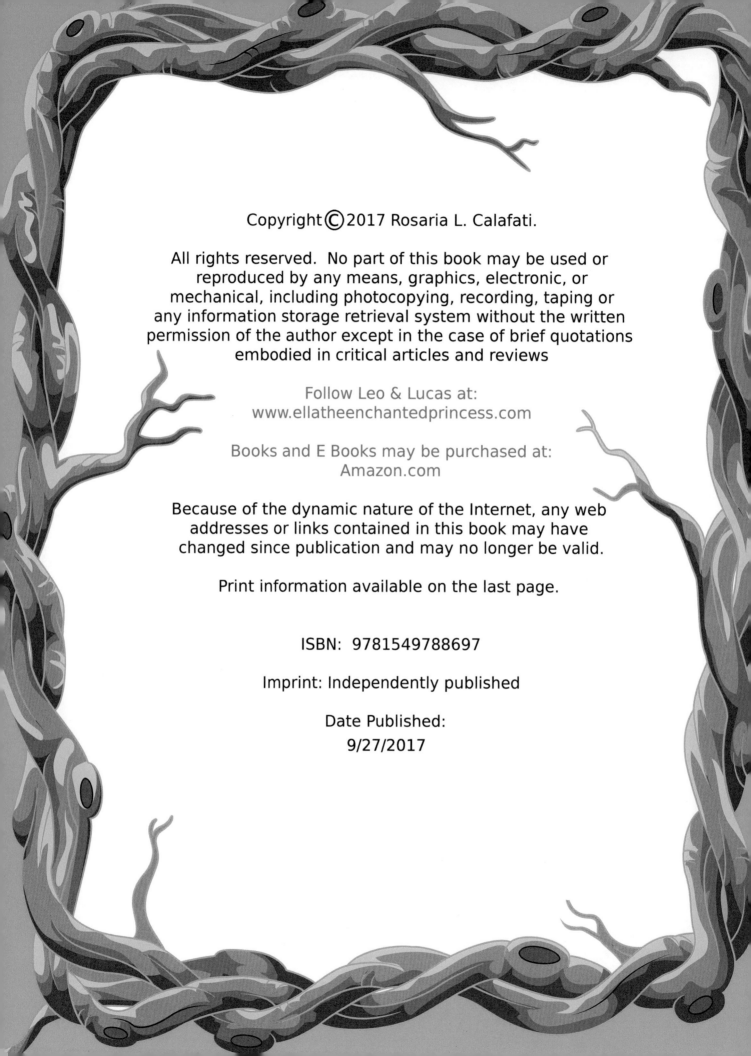

Follow Leo & Lucas at:
www.ellatheenchantedprincess.com

Books and E Books may be purchased at:
Amazon.com

Because of the dynamic nature of the Internet, any web addresses or links contained in this book may have changed since publication and may no longer be valid.

Print information available on the last page.

ISBN: 9781549788697

Imprint: Independently published

Date Published:
9/27/2017

This book is dedicated to

MY WONDERFUL HUSBAND PETER

Babe, my life would have
never been this happy if you
had not been there to save me.

You have been by my side through
good and bad and together we
make a fantastic team!

Thank you for your love and for
supporting me in whatever
I choose to do!

I love you with all my heart
and I can never
imagine my life without you.

Love You,
Rosaria

Way up high in the mountains of the
Enchanted Forest lived a little boy named
Leo. He lived with his Mom and Dad on a
farm far away from the town of Faylin.
The only people he knew were his parents.
His only friends were the animals on the
farm and the animals in the mountains.

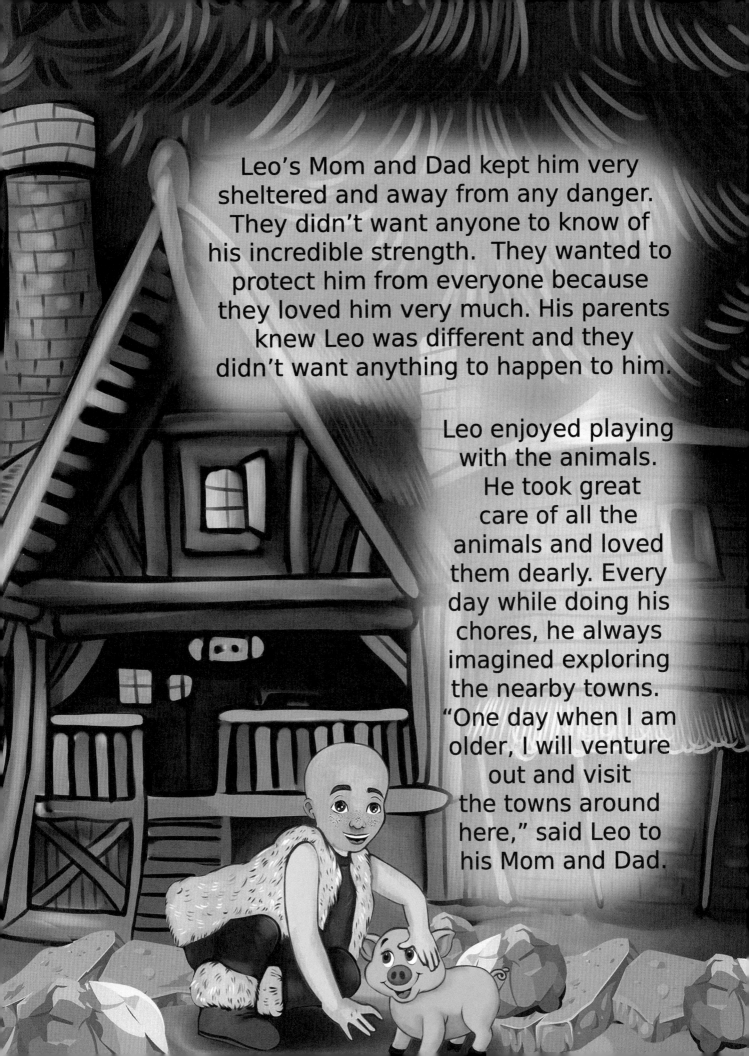

Leo's Mom and Dad kept him very sheltered and away from any danger. They didn't want anyone to know of his incredible strength. They wanted to protect him from everyone because they loved him very much. His parents knew Leo was different and they didn't want anything to happen to him.

Leo enjoyed playing with the animals. He took great care of all the animals and loved them dearly. Every day while doing his chores, he always imagined exploring the nearby towns. "One day when I am older, I will venture out and visit the towns around here," said Leo to his Mom and Dad.

Leo was a different little boy. He was kind and gentle and cared a lot about the things that surrounded him. Leo was born with no hair. Not having hair never bothered him. Although Leo was young, he had a lot of strength for a little boy. He had big hands and feet, and some might say he looked a little clumsy. Leo was mighty, but he was kind and gentle too.

Leo didn't realize how much strength he had. Leo thought that he was just like any other boy. He always dreamed of joining the kingdom's army and fighting for what is right. "How can I do this when I am stuck here in the mountains?" Leo thought out loud.

Leo worked very hard on the farm with his Mom and Dad and had very little time to play.

Because of his strength, he could do the job of many men and never get tired. He helped his father when he planted the land.

Leo loved working on the farm, especially taking care of the animals.

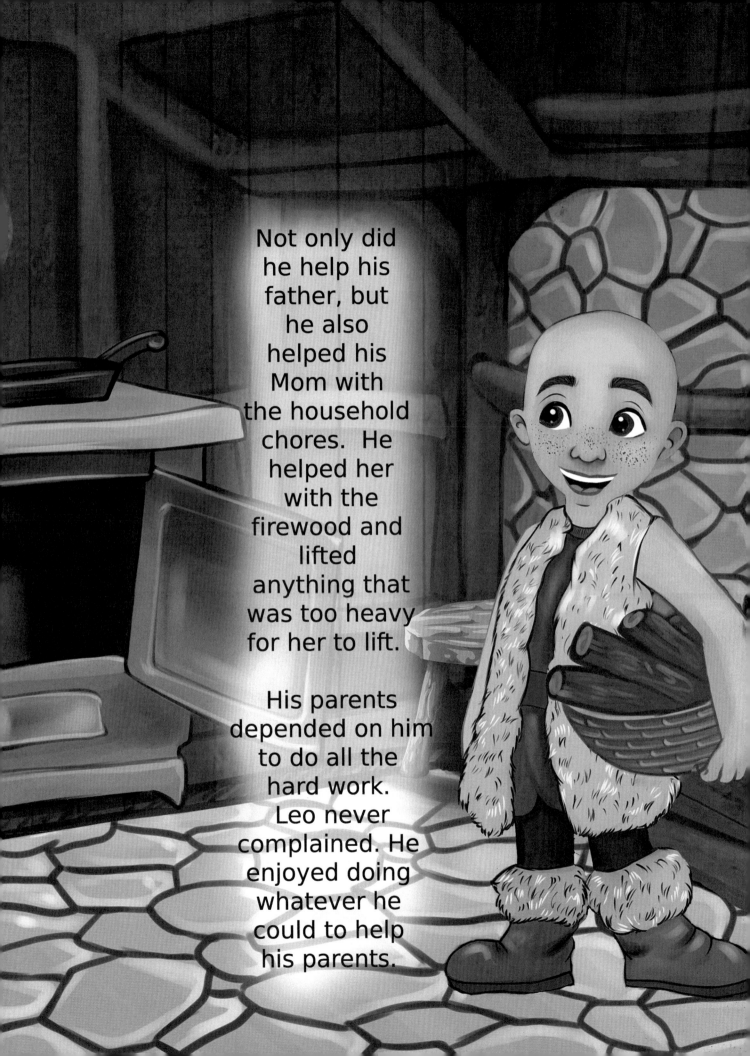

Not only did he help his father, but he also helped his Mom with the household chores. He helped her with the firewood and lifted anything that was too heavy for her to lift.

His parents depended on him to do all the hard work. Leo never complained. He enjoyed doing whatever he could to help his parents.

After a long day of work, Leo would go into the barn and play. He had a few toys made of wood that he loved dearly. His favorite toy was a wooden sword that his Dad gave him. His father carved a wooden shield to match his sword out of a majestic tree that was in the Enchanted Forest.

In his spare time, he played with his sword and shield and pretended that he was helping people all over the world.

Leo always made believe he was saving people from falling rocks or flying dragons. He imagined himself as a warrior ready to fight and save the day. He would wear a bucket on his head like a helmet and a cape that his Mom made for him. Dressing up like a warrior made Leo feel very important. He took great care of his few toys. He always made sure to put them away neatly in the corner of the barn.

Every day, Leo would walk with the flock of sheep on the side of the mountain. "I love being here with you," said Leo to the sheep. He enjoyed being outside and playing with these peaceful animals.

While Leo was tending the flock, there was a noise coming from the forest. He never heard this kind of sound before.

"I think someone is crying," Leo said. "Who can it be? Someone needs my help! I am going to slowly walk up the hill to find out what is making this noise." Leo was a little afraid of what he would see. Leo knew that no matter what animal was hurt, he had to help it.

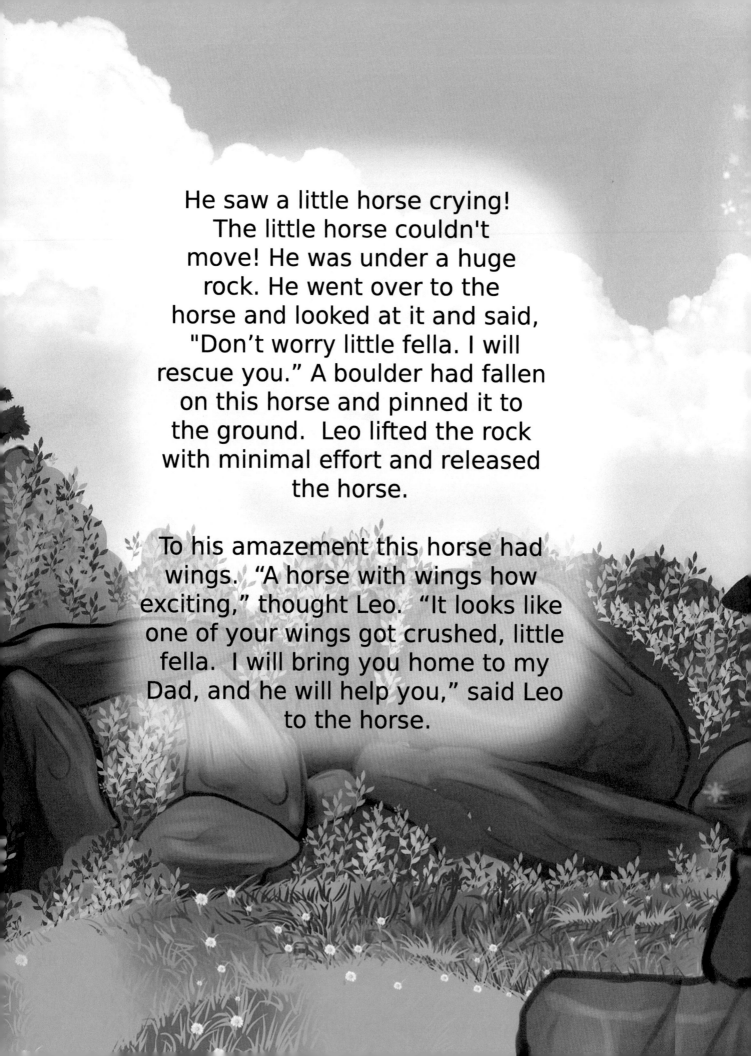

He saw a little horse crying! The little horse couldn't move! He was under a huge rock. He went over to the horse and looked at it and said, "Don't worry little fella. I will rescue you." A boulder had fallen on this horse and pinned it to the ground. Leo lifted the rock with minimal effort and released the horse.

To his amazement this horse had wings. "A horse with wings how exciting," thought Leo. "It looks like one of your wings got crushed, little fella. I will bring you home to my Dad, and he will help you," said Leo to the horse.

With no hesitation, he scooped up
the horse in his arms and ran home
to his father.

"Dad, I rescued this horse. He was
stuck under a rock. He has a crushed wing,
please help him," said Leo. His Dad strangely
looked at the horse.

"What's wrong Dad?" asked Leo.
"Flying horses are white, but this
one is pure black," said Dad.
"He must be an extraordinary horse,"
said Leo. Dad just sighed as he
wrapped the animal's wing very tight
to his body.

"Leo, you will need to care for this
horse and nurture him back to health.
But once he gets his strength back and
can fly, you have to let him go,"
said Dad. "He needs to go back to his
family of flying horses." Leo was
sad that he had to let him go,
but he understood. Leo was ready
to take care of the horse.

The next few months were the best in Leo's life. He took care of the flying horse.

"I will call you Lucas," said Leo to the horse. He was not an ordinary horse, but a clumsy-looking one. He had the face of a donkey. And then there were those tiny wings. The horse's features didn't bother Leo. He thought that Lucas was beautiful no matter what. With each passing day, Lucas grew stronger and bigger. Leo couldn't believe how mighty Lucas became.

"It is time to let your horse go now. He must return to his family. He does not belong here," said Dad. Although Leo was very sad, he knew he had to let him go.

He went over to Lucas and told him, "Today is the day I have to let you go to join your family." Lucas looked at Leo and wasn't sure what to do. He didn't know anyone but Leo.

"Fly away, Lucas. It is your time to go with the other horses and play in the sky," said Leo with tears in his eyes. "You are the only one I know. You are my family! I don't want to go back to the flying horses," said Lucas. "I love you and want to stay with you."

Leo walked away from Lucas in
hopes that he would fly away.
But Lucas kept following him.
No matter what Leo did, Lucas
kept coming back. Leo knew he
had to let him go, because he
promised his father that he would.

After trying many ways to get Lucas
to leave, he had to tell his father
that Lucas would not fly away.
With great hesitation, his father let
Lucas stay and live with them.

Leo and Lucas became perfect
friends. They were inseparable.
Together they got in and out of
trouble. Lucas would even
crawl into Leo's room and
sleep with him.

Leo loves to mount Lucas and ride him. He loves flying high in the sky. His favorite thing to do with Lucas is swooping in and out of the clouds and he especially likes racing with the birds.

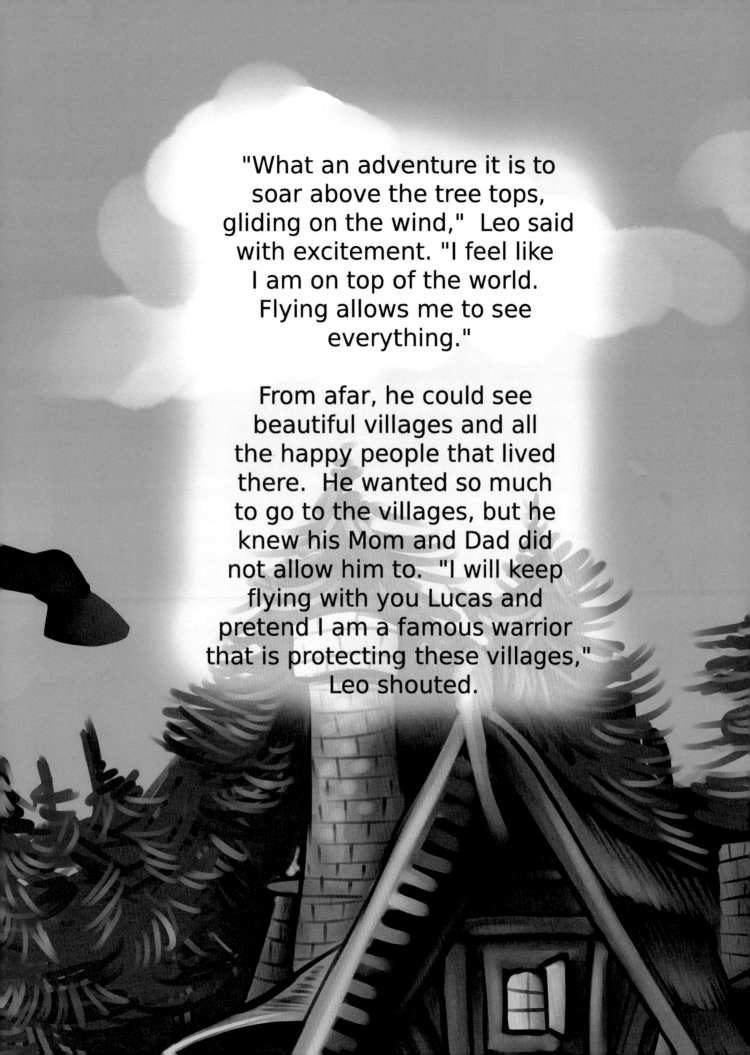

"What an adventure it is to soar above the tree tops, gliding on the wind," Leo said with excitement. "I feel like I am on top of the world. Flying allows me to see everything."

From afar, he could see beautiful villages and all the happy people that lived there. He wanted so much to go to the villages, but he knew his Mom and Dad did not allow him to. "I will keep flying with you Lucas and pretend I am a famous warrior that is protecting these villages," Leo shouted.

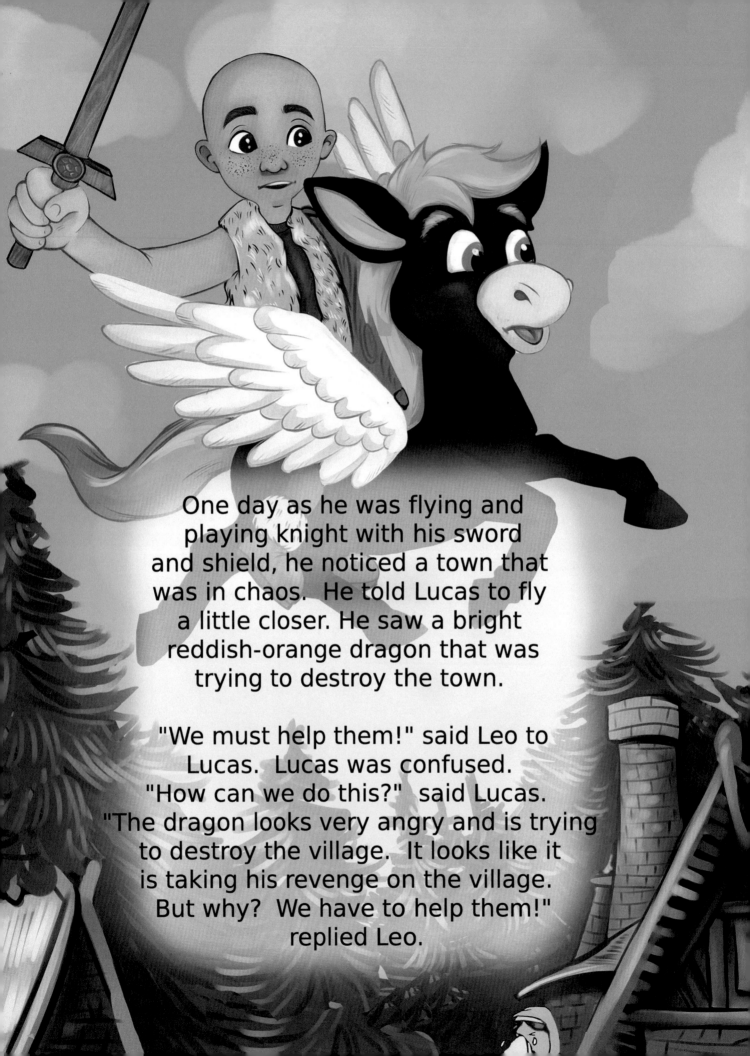

One day as he was flying and
playing knight with his sword
and shield, he noticed a town that
was in chaos. He told Lucas to fly
a little closer. He saw a bright
reddish-orange dragon that was
trying to destroy the town.

"We must help them!" said Leo to
Lucas. Lucas was confused.
"How can we do this?" said Lucas.
"The dragon looks very angry and is trying
to destroy the village. It looks like it
is taking his revenge on the village.
But why? We have to help them!"
replied Leo.

Waving his sword, Leo and Lucas swooped in trying to distract the dragon. The mighty dragon roared with anger.

"Lucas, we have to help the town before their whole village is burnt down. Let's go after the dragon!" yelled Leo.

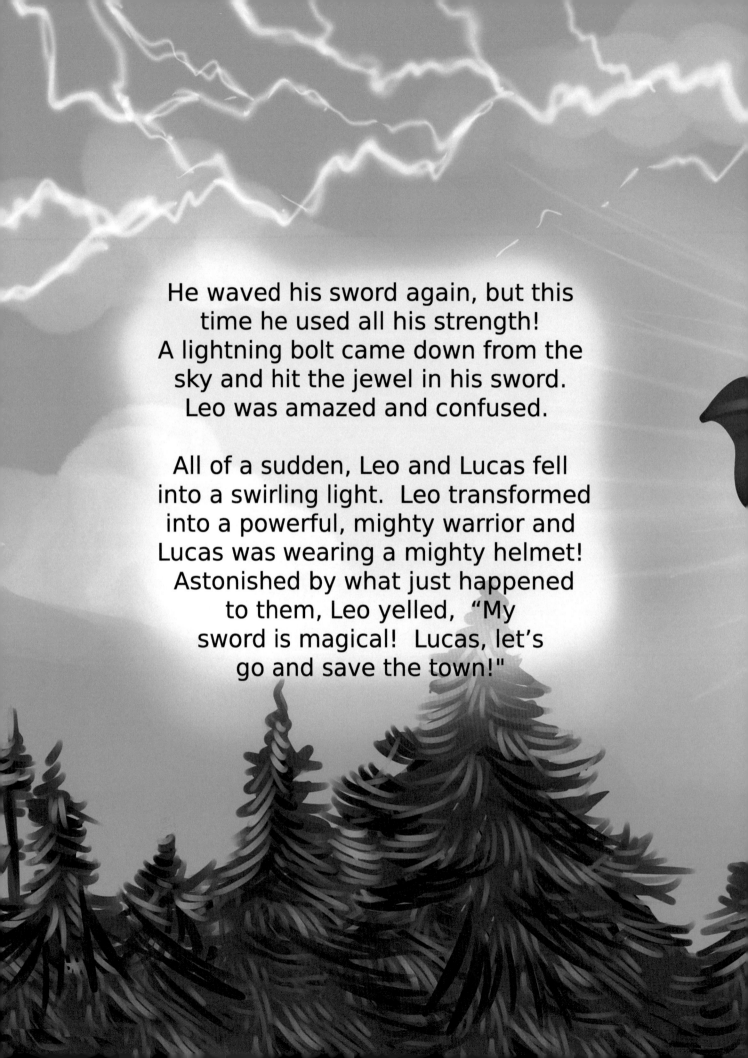

He waved his sword again, but this
time he used all his strength!
A lightning bolt came down from the
sky and hit the jewel in his sword.
Leo was amazed and confused.

All of a sudden, Leo and Lucas fell
into a swirling light. Leo transformed
into a powerful, mighty warrior and
Lucas was wearing a mighty helmet!
Astonished by what just happened
to them, Leo yelled, "My
sword is magical! Lucas, let's
go and save the town!"

Hundreds of thousands of soldiers
from the town's army were trying to
shoot the dragon with arrows. As Leo
dove in and out of the arrows he said,
"It's no use taking the dragon down.
It's invincible. Absolutely nothing
can hold it back."

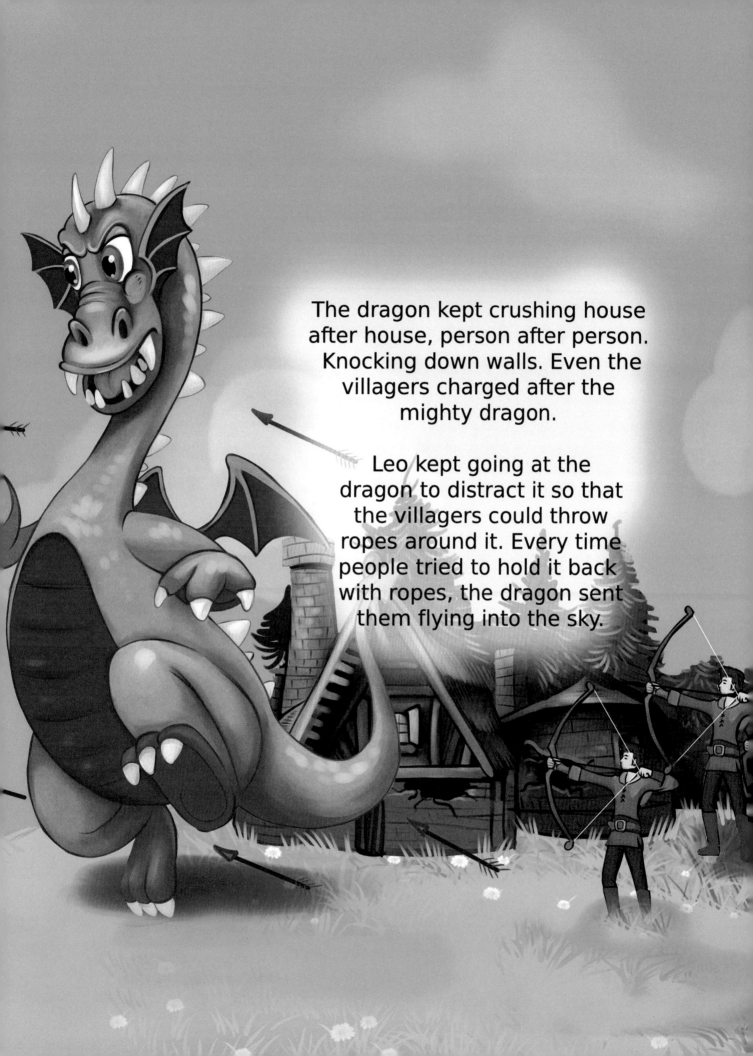

The dragon kept crushing house after house, person after person. Knocking down walls. Even the villagers charged after the mighty dragon.

Leo kept going at the dragon to distract it so that the villagers could throw ropes around it. Every time people tried to hold it back with ropes, the dragon sent them flying into the sky.

Leo tried waving his sword again, aiming it at the dragon. A spark of fire flew toward the dragon. "Wow!" said Leo. "Let's fight fire with fire!" He did it again and again until the dragon gave up and decided to leave.

Leo screamed to Lucas, "Watch out!
The dragon is flying over our heads!"
Its giant wings made a loud swooshing
sound. Lucas quickly darted out
of the dragon's path. As they watched
the dragon fly away, they decided to
secretly follow it to its den.

Leo and Lucas got closer
to the cave and the dragon
began to roar at them! The dragon
was warning them to stay away!
There in the den were dragon eggs
which had hatched.

The mother dragon came at Leo with brute force trying to attack him! Leo raised his shield and sword and charged the dragon and started to attack her! Lucas yelled, "Leo, stop! You are the protector of all animals! Do not harm the dragon or her children."

Leo put his sword down and said to the dragon,
"I don't want to harm you or your babies. But
why are you attacking the town?" "They want to take
my babies away from me and I will do anything to
protect my children," said the dragon.

While Leo talked to the dragon, he realized she
didn't want to hurt anyone. She was very
kind and gentle. The dragon loved her
babies very much. She said, "I don't want to
hurt people, but they were attacking me first.
I was just protecting myself and my children!"
Leo knew he had to help the dragon.
"I will help you protect your babies," Leo said.

Leo decided that he was going back to the village
to convince the villagers not to go after the dragon's
babies. He told them that the dragon was kind
and was attacking because she was trying
to protect her babies. He also told them that
the dragon will protect them too!

After convincing the villagers to leave the dragon
and her babies alone, Leo and Lucas headed home.
While flying toward his house, they slowly changed
back into their usual selves.

Leo went home to tell his Dad of the tale of the dragon. He was so excited to tell him about his sword.

"Dad, while I was flying a bolt of lightning struck my sword and we changed into fighting warriors. I saved a town from a fire-breathing dragon. I also helped the dragon and her babies."

Leo was very excited but confused.
"Why is all of this happening to me?"
Leo asked his Dad. "It was ony a matter
of time before you unlocked the powers
of the sword," his father replied. "What
do you mean?" It is only a wooden toy
sword," Leo said.

His father started to explain what was happening to Leo. "Many years ago when I was walking through the Enchanted Forest, I stumbled upon a flock of flying horses. The Queen of the flying horses stopped me. She gave me a wooden sword. She told me that she made the sword from the purest wood found from the strongest tree in the Enchanted Forest. She placed a unique green emerald in the sword. This jewel came from the darkest caves of the forest. I looked at her, baffled. I didn't know why she was giving me this sword. She said that I was to save this sword in a safe place and not use it."

Leo and Lucas were still confused. His father continued telling him what the Queen said. "She said that one day I would have

a son that would be an extraordinary little boy.That was you! She said I should give this sword to him and one day a black flying horse will be born amongst us.

Fate will bring them together. This horse will become your son's best friend. Nurture them both since they will become the greatest warriors that all humankind will know. The powers of the sword will unfold only when your son is in danger. Until then he can play with it as an ordinary toy."

"We kept you away from everyone because we didn't want any danger to find you. But the day you brought Lucas home I knew your life was going to change! Together you will help people all over the world. But first, you have to learn how to use this very special sword and embrace your strength!"

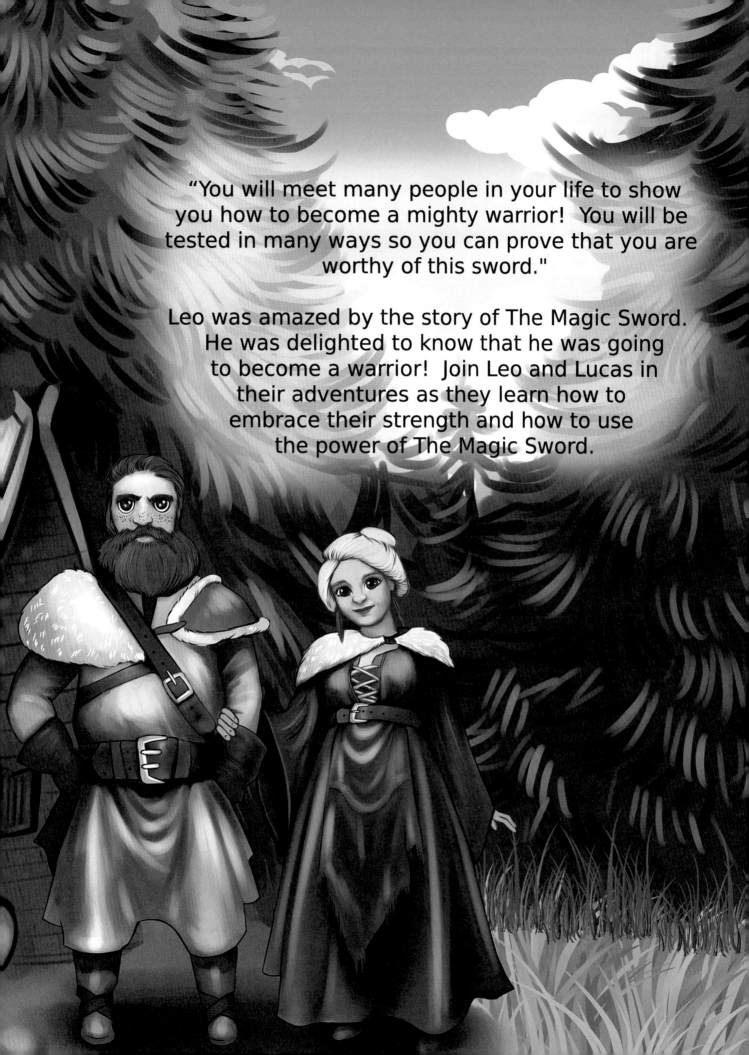

"You will meet many people in your life to show you how to become a mighty warrior! You will be tested in many ways so you can prove that you are worthy of this sword."

Leo was amazed by the story of The Magic Sword. He was delighted to know that he was going to become a warrior! Join Leo and Lucas in their adventures as they learn how to embrace their strength and how to use the power of The Magic Sword.

ABOUT THE AUTHOR

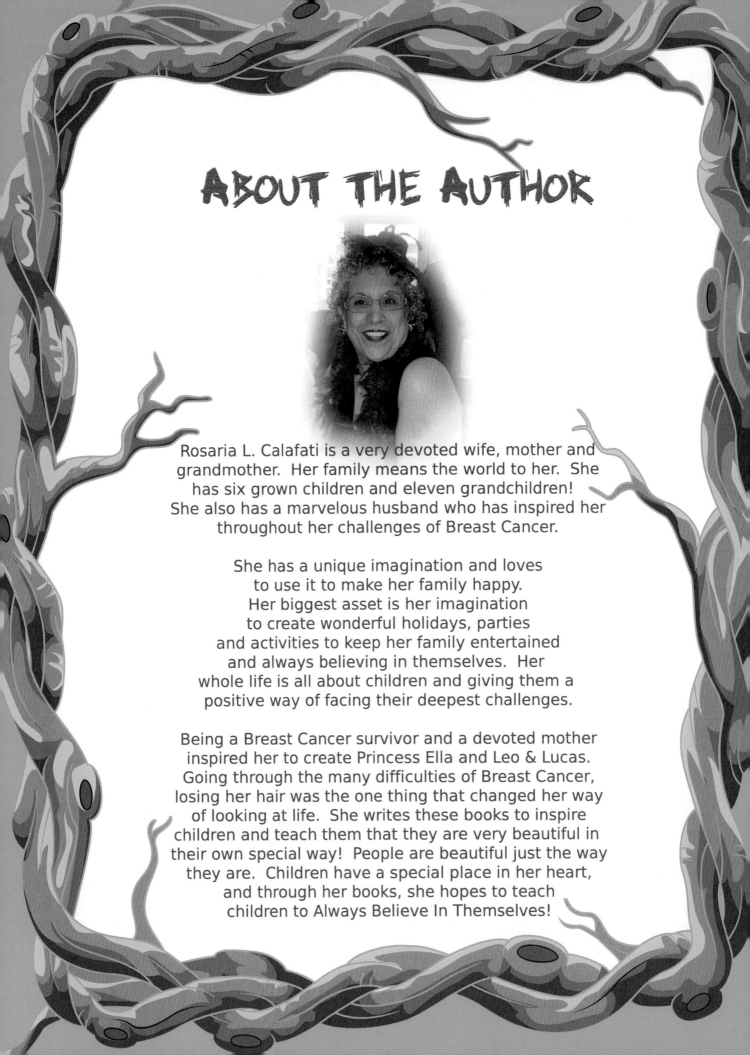

Rosaria L. Calafati is a very devoted wife, mother and grandmother. Her family means the world to her. She has six grown children and eleven grandchildren! She also has a marvelous husband who has inspired her throughout her challenges of Breast Cancer.

She has a unique imagination and loves to use it to make her family happy. Her biggest asset is her imagination to create wonderful holidays, parties and activities to keep her family entertained and always believing in themselves. Her whole life is all about children and giving them a positive way of facing their deepest challenges.

Being a Breast Cancer survivor and a devoted mother inspired her to create Princess Ella and Leo & Lucas. Going through the many difficulties of Breast Cancer, losing her hair was the one thing that changed her way of looking at life. She writes these books to inspire children and teach them that they are very beautiful in their own special way! People are beautiful just the way they are. Children have a special place in her heart, and through her books, she hopes to teach children to Always Believe In Themselves!